Dear Parents:

Congratulations! Your child is taking the first steps on an exciting journey. The destination? Independent reading!

STEP INTO READING® will help your child get there. The program offers five steps to reading success. Each step includes fun stories and colorful art or photographs. In addition to original fiction and books with favorite characters, there are Step into Reading Non-Fiction Readers, Phonics Readers and Boxed Sets, Sticker Readers, and Comic Readers—a complete literacy program with something to interest every child.

Learning to Read, Step by Step!

Ready to Read   Preschool–Kindergarten
• big type and easy words • rhyme and rhythm • picture clues
For children who know the alphabet and are eager to begin reading.

Reading with Help   Preschool–Grade 1
• basic vocabulary • short sentences • simple stories
For children who recognize familiar words and sound out new words with help.

Reading on Your Own   Grades 1–3
• engaging characters • easy-to-follow plots • popular topics
For children who are ready to read on their own.

Reading Paragraphs   Grades 2–3
• challenging vocabulary • short paragraphs • exciting stories
For newly independent readers who read simple sentences with confidence.

Ready for Chapters   Grades 2–4
• chapters • longer paragraphs • full-color art
For children who want to take the plunge into chapter books but still like colorful pictures.

STEP INTO READING® is designed to give every child a successful reading experience. The grade levels are only guides; children will progress through the steps at their own speed, developing confidence in their reading.

Remember, a lifetime love of reading starts with a single step!

Step into Reading, Random House, and the Random House colophon are registered trademarks of Penguin Random House LLC.

Visit us on the Web!
StepIntoReading.com
rhcbooks.com

Educators and librarians, for a variety of teaching tools, visit us at RHTeachersLibrarians.com

ISBN 978-0-7364-4337-1 (trade)

MANUFACTURED IN CHINA

10 9 8 7 6 5 4 3 2 1

Disney PRINCESS

palace pets

Perfect
Princess Pets!

A Collection of Six Early Readers

Random House 🏠 New York

Contents

DISNEY PRINCESS
palace pets

Rapunzel's Perfect Pony

adapted by Lauren Clauss

illustrated by the Disney Storybook Art Team

Random House 🏠 New York

Meet Blondie!

She is Rapunzel's
royal pony.

When Blondie was small,
she dreamed of being
a royal pony.

She liked

the pretty saddles.

One day,

she joined a royal parade.

Rapunzel loved
the little pony!

Now Blondie lives in
the castle with Rapunzel.

Blondie is friends with
Summer and Meadow.

Blondie loves it when
Rapunzel brushes
her mane.

She also loves to play
with Flynn!

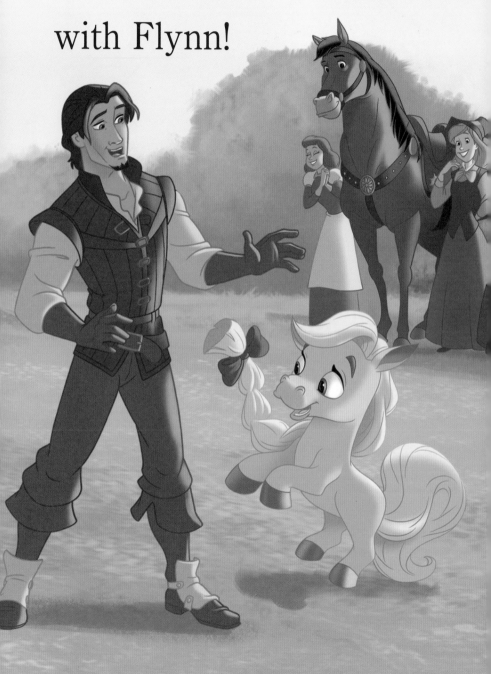

The other horses
tell Blondie that
Rapunzel is getting
a new pet named Daisy.

Blondie is sad.
She likes being
the new pet!

Blondie thinks about
how happy she is
with Rapunzel.

Pascal tells
Blondie that Daisy
should be happy, too!

Blondie agrees.

She collects apples

for Daisy to eat.

She finds a warm place
for Daisy to sleep.

Blondie meets Daisy.

Daisy is nice!

Blondie is happy
for her new friend.

Blondie is
Rapunzel's
perfect pony!

Ariel's Brave Kitten

by Amy Sky Koster

illustrated by the Disney Storybook Art Team

Random House 🏠 New York

Meet Treasure!

Treasure is a kitten.

She loves the sea!

One day, Treasure climbed
onto Prince Eric's boat.

Treasure took a nap.

The crew found her!

Prince Eric liked
the small kitten!

Treasure helped put flowers on the ship for a special guest.

Princess Ariel
was the guest!
Treasure was excited.

Ariel loved Treasure.

Treasure became Ariel's kitten!

Treasure loves to play
at the beach
with her friends.

They find a boat.

They play in the boat.

A big wave
carries the boat
out to sea!

Treasure is happy.

Her friends are worried.

It starts to rain.

Treasure is scared.

The rain stops.

There is a rainbow!

A wave brings the boat
back to shore.

Eric and Ariel arrive.

They see Treasure

in the boat.

They are glad

the kitten is safe!

Treasure is Ariel's brave kitten!

DISNEY
PRINCESS

palace
pets

Mulan's Happy Panda

by Amy Sky Koster

illustrated by the Disney Storybook Art Team

Random House 🏠 New York

Blossom is a panda.

Her tummy rumbles.

She is hungry.

Blossom runs
to a nearby town.

She crawls under
the gate.

The town is
having a party!
It is the Moon Festival.

Blossom sees tables

covered with food.

She reaches

for something to eat.

Someone scares her.

She runs away!

Blossom runs into
the crowd.
She hides under
a cloth dragon.

Blossom dances

in the parade!

But everyone leaves
when they see Blossom.
They are afraid
of bears!

Blossom finds more food.

Mulan is at the table!

Mulan and Blossom
both reach for cake.
The cakes fall!

Mulan looks at Blossom.
She thinks the panda
is very cute!

Mulan picks Blossom up.

She invites Blossom
to live with her!

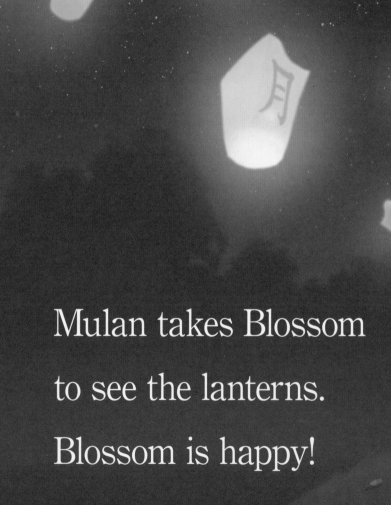

Mulan takes Blossom

to see the lanterns.

Blossom is happy!

Blossom

loves Mulan!

DISNEY PRINCESS

Palace Pets

Belle's Playful Puppy

by Amy Sky Koster

illustrated by the Disney Storybook Art Team

Random House 🏠 New York

Meet Teacup!

She is a puppy.

She puts on a show.

People clap.

The people give
Teacup treats!

Princess Belle
sees Teacup.

The sun is bright.

It gets in Teacup's eyes.

Teacup drops her cup.

She is sad.

Belle helps Teacup.

Teacup hugs Belle.

She likes the princess!

Belle takes Teacup home.

Teacup is her new pet!

Soon, Teacup is ready
to do her show again.

She runs toward
the town.
She goes through
the woods.

She makes new friends
in the woods.

Teacup puts on a show
for her new friends!

Teacup is ready to go
to the town.

She gets lost!

Teacup hears a noise.

She is scared.

It is Petit!

She is looking for Teacup.

Petit gives Teacup glasses.
They will block the sun!

Petit takes Teacup
to the town square.

Teacup and Petit put on
a great show together!

Teacup has many
new friends.
Hooray!

DISNEY PRINCESS

palace pets

Snow White's Sweet Bunny

by Lauren Clauss

illustrated by the Disney Storybook Art Team

Random House 🏠 New York

Meet Berry.

She is Snow White's bunny!

One day,
Snow White and
the Prince went for
a walk.

Snow White heard a noise.

It came from a bush.

It was Berry!

Snow White fed her.

Berry followed

the princess home.

Now Berry is

a royal bunny!

She wears a special crown.

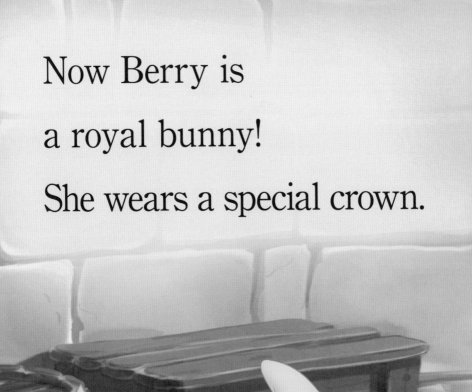

She eats blueberry pie every day!

Berry needs water.

She goes to the well.

She hops

into the bucket.

The bucket swings away
from the ledge.

Berry is stuck!

Sweetie is Berry's friend.

She sees Berry's ears

in the bucket.

Sweetie pulls Berry
back to safety.

Berry is thankful!
She hugs Sweetie.

Berry and Sweetie
run home.
Snow White makes
a pie for them!

Berry and Sweetie
love being Palace Pets!

Disney
PRINCESS

Palace
Pets

Tiana's Kind Pony

by Amy Sky Koster

illustrated by the Disney Storybook Art Team

Random House New York

Meet Bayou!

She is a pony.

Naveen's parents

give Bayou

to Princess Tiana.

There is a parade
in the town.
Tiana finds Bayou
a costume.

Bayou is shy.

Tiana gives Bayou

a piece of pie.

Yummy!

Tiana takes Bayou
to the parade.
Bayou is happy!

They sit in Tiana's car
and watch the parade.

Now Bayou and Tiana
join the parade.
The crowd cheers.
Bayou has fun!

The next day,
Bayou meets Charlotte.
Charlotte loves
Tiana's kind pony!

Tiana takes Bayou
to Tiana's Palace.
It is Bayou's
favorite place!

Bayou goes with Tiana
to work every day.

She plays with
her friend Lily.

Naveen tells Tiana
that Louis is missing.
Louis plays the trumpet.
The band cannot play
without Louis!

Bayou and Lily will help!

They search for Louis.

Lily's tail brushes
some leaves.
Swish, swish, swish!

Bayou's hooves tap
on the sidewalk.
Tap, tap, tap!

Bayou and Lily
find Louis's house.

Louis is asleep!

Swish, tap. Swish, tap.

Louis hears Lily
and Bayou.

He wakes up!

Louis jumps out of bed.
He grabs his trumpet.
It is time to go!

They all run back
to Tiana's Palace.

Tiana is happy.

Now the band can play!

Tiana thanks
Bayou and Lily.
They are her kind
Palace Pets!